*Charles M. Schulz* (signature)

# Sally's Christmas Play

## Charles M. Schulz

**HarperHorizon**
*An Imprint of HarperCollinsPublishers*

First published in 1998 by HarperCollins*Publishers* Inc. http://www.harpercollins.com. Copyright © 1998 United Feature Syndicate, Inc. All rights reserved. HarperCollins ® and ▲ ® are trademarks of HarperCollins*Publishers* Inc. *Sally's Christmas Play* was published by HarperHorizon, an imprint of HarperCollins*Publishers* Inc., 10 East 53rd Street, New York, NY 10022. Horizon is a registered trademark used under license from Forbes Inc. PEANUTS is a registered trademark of United Feature Syndicate, Inc. PEANUTS © United Feature Syndicate, Inc. Based on the PEANUTS ® comic strip by Charles M. Schulz. http://www.unitedmedia.com. ISBN 0-694-01077-4. Printed in Hong Kong.

"Guess what, big brother—I've been
asked to be in the Christmas play!"

"I'm going to be an angel. All I have to do is say 'Hark!'"

"This is what I have to do in the play . . . when the sheep are through dancing, I come out and say, 'Hark!' Then Harold Angel starts to sing."

"Harold Angel?" said Charlie Brown.

"It's right here in the script . . ."

"I'm afraid of getting out on the stage and forgetting what I'm supposed to say."

"Well, if you did, you could always make up something."

"That's true. . . . How about, 'Hey!' "

"Not very biblical."

"I'm all set for the play.
Do I look like an angel?"

"You look fine, Sally. Are you going to walk to the auditorium like that? Can you get your coat on over your wings?"

"No problem."

"So far this has been a good
    Christmas play, Charlie Brown.
    When does your sister come on?"

"Right after the dancing sheep she steps out and says 'Hark!' and then Harold Angel sings."

"Harold Angel?"

"All I know is what she told me."

"The sheep are through dancing,
Charlie Brown. Here comes your
sister . . ."

"'HOCKEY STICK!'?"

"I said 'Hockey Stick!' Why did I say 'Hockey Stick!'? All I had to say was 'Hark!' . . .

. . . and I said 'Hockey Stick!'"

"I don't know, Linus, I didn't see the rest of the play. As soon as Sally said 'Hockey Stick!' I left. She gets everything mixed up. She even thought someone named 'Harold Angel' was going to sing!"

"Hi, is Sally home? My name is Harold Angel."